Monster
in the
Mirror

Monster
in the
Mirror

JEAN URE

Illustrated by Doffy Weir

Collins

An imprint of HarperCollins*Publishers*

For Pat and Muffy
(with apologies to Muffy)

First published in Great Britain by Collins in 2000
Collins is an imprint of HarperCollins*Publishers* Ltd
77-85 Fulham Palace Road, Hammersmith, London W6 8JB

ISBN 978-0-00-675531-9

The HarperCollins website address is www.**fire**and**water**.com

Text copyright © Jean Ure 2000
Illustrations copyright © Doffy Weir 2000

The author and illustrator assert the moral right
be identified as author and illustrator of the worl

JS

CHAPTER ONE

This is the story of Woffles and Stretch. Woffles was a dog, very big and woolly. Stretch was a cat, very smooth and slinky.

Stretch was called Stretch because he liked to stre-e-e-e-e-tch.

Upwards, downwards, even backwards in a circle. He was a very stretchy sort of cat.

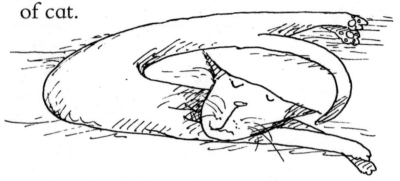

Woffles was called Woffles because he liked to woffle. He woffled round the garden. He woffled round the park. He was a real woffle hound.

Woffles and Stretch lived in a house with their People. Woffles and Stretch loved their People and their People loved them. Everybody was happy until one day…

"See what we have here!" cried the People.

Woffles was asleep on the sofa. He woke up at once and went running to look.

Stretch was asleep on top of the washing machine. He opened an eye.

What had the People brought home? Was it food?

No!

Woffles screeched to a halt.

What was it?

It was in a basket, on the kitchen table. A small black bundle of fur. It was a cat!

"Poor little thing," said the People, waggling their fingers. "She has no People. Come and say hello!"

Stretch leapt off the washing
machine. He picked his way slowly,
slo-o-o-o-wly, across the kitchen
floor.

Woffles crept
after him. Woffles
wasn't very brave.

"Tsssss!" went the cat, showing its claws.

Woffles sprang backwards in alarm. All his fur stood on end. He looked like a lavatory brush.

Stretch stayed where he was. He arched his back, in a U bend.

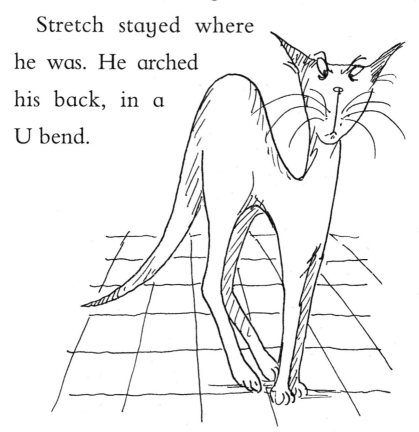

"Watch it!" he hissed. No strange cat came into *his* house and spat at him.

"Now, Stretch," said the People. "Don't be like that! Can't you see she's frightened?"

The new cat didn't
look frightened.

Woffles was frightened!
He stood in the corner,
shaking.

"What a big baby," laughed the People. "You're twice the size of this poor little mite!"

The poor little mite held up a claw. All its nails were stuck out like pins on a pincushion.

"I wish it hadn't come,"
thought Woffles.

Stretch just glinted, out of his green
eyes. That cat had better behave or
there would be TROUBLE.

CHAPTER TWO

The new cat was called Muffy. Her manners were quite dreadful.

She spat and she hissed. She hissed and she spat. She grumbled and growled. She made poor Woffles' life a misery.

She didn't hiss or spit at the People.
Oh, no! She was too clever for that.
She sat on the People's laps and
purred. She jumped on the People's
shoulders and rubbed her face against
theirs. The People thought she was a
real sweetie!

Muffy didn't hiss at Stretch, either. She tried it just once, but Stretch spat back, and bopped her with his paw. "Watch it!" he hissed.

Muffy didn't like it when Stretch bopped her. So she left him alone and went to spit at Woffles, instead.

Woffles was such a big softie. Muffy bullied him all day long.

She lay in wait for him, in dark corners. She snatched at his tail. She clawed at his ears. Woffles couldn't eat his dinner in peace.

He couldn't lie on the sofa and snooze.

He couldn't even woffle about the garden, smelling interesting smells.

Poor Woffles! He was very unhappy. He didn't wag, he didn't play. He didn't do any of the doggy things that he had done before. He just hid beneath the kitchen table, or sat trembling in the garden, too scared to come in.

The People told him he was a big
daft mutt. "Fancy being scared of a
little thing like that!"

Muffy became quite puffed up. She paraded about the house with her tail in the air and a wicked grin on her face. All the time she was planning new ways to torment poor Woffles…

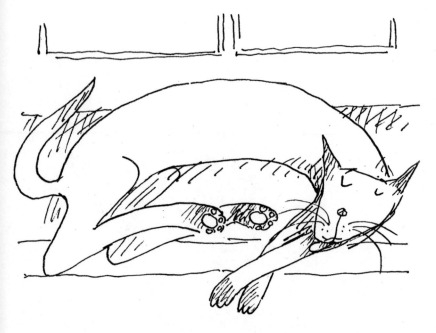

As for Stretch, he just slept and ate,
and groomed and stretched, and didn't
lift a paw. Why should he? He was all
right! Nobody was bullying him.

CHAPTER THREE

One Sunday, the People went to visit friends. "Be good," they told the animals. "We'll be back at dinner time."

The People jumped in their car and drove off.

Woffles watched through the window.
He didn't like it when the People were
out. He didn't feel safe all on his own
with Muffy.

Stretch didn't mind. He was happy snoozing on top of the television. He was going to snooze until dinner time.

Woffles jumped down from the window seat. He looked round, nervously, for Muffy. Where was she?

She was nowhere to be seen. Was she shut in a cupboard? Was she locked in the garage? Maybe she had gone away!

Woffles clambered on to the sofa. He gave a deep sigh and settled down to sleep. He was in the middle of a beautiful dream when…

SCREEEEEEEECH!

Something dropped on him.
Something round. And black.
And prickly. Something like
a big furry pincushion...

Woffles gave a yelp of terror and sprang off the sofa. The pincushion sprang after him, green eyes gleaming. Chase the dog ! Get the dog!

Woffles ran into the hall. The pincushion ran after him. Its green eyes gleamed. Chase the dog! Get the dog!

Woffles went tearing out into the hall. The pincushion tore after him.

Bang! went Woffles'
head against the leg of
the hall table.

Thud! went Woffles' heart against
his rib cage.

Woffles raced into the kitchen. He was terrified! He squeezed himself between the washing machine and the fridge. But even there he wasn't safe.

The pincushion leapt on to the washing machine and began slashing at him from above.

Woffles howled and tore back again. Up the hall, into the sitting room. Round the sofa, round the chairs. Chased by a spitting bundle of fur…

And Stretch just opened an eye, and closed it again, and went on snoozing. It was nothing to do with him. He wasn't the one being bullied.

But it was hard to sleep with such a noise going on. Thud, thump! Bang, bump!

Tinkle, smash! Wallop, crash!

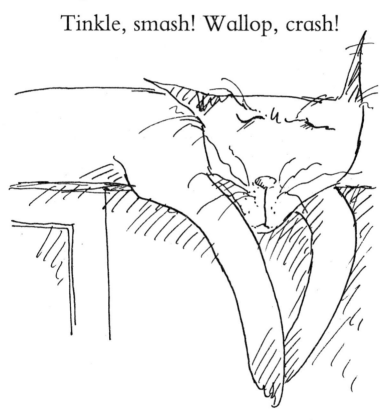

Stretch twitched his whiskers, crossly. This was impossible!

Suddenly, everything went quiet.
Stretch opened an eye.

Muffy was sitting on the sofa. She
was washing herself, and looking very
pleased.

Stretch stood up, on top of the television set. He yawned and he stretched. He stretched and he yawned. Then he leapt to the floor and went strolling out. He was king of this house!

But where was Woffles?

Woffles was under the kitchen table.
Woffles was too scared to come out.
He was shaking all over, like a jelly.

"This is not good enough," said Stretch. "A cat can have no peace in this house! It is nothing but noise from morning to night."

Woffles hung his head.

"It is not your fault," said Stretch. "You are only a dog, after all. It takes a cat to deal with a cat. Leave it to me! I shall put a stop to this nonsense once and for all."

"But how?" whimpered Woffles.

"You'll see," said Stretch. He waved a paw. "Come along now! Come with me."

CHAPTER FOUR

Woffles crawled out from under the kitchen table. He was still frightened.

"Follow me," said Stretch.

Stretch led the way back up the hall. Woffles crept behind. His legs had gone all wobbly.

Muffy was still sitting on the sofa, washing herself.

"I suppose you think you are really big and fierce?" said Stretch.

Muffy smirked, and went on washing.

"Well, let me tell you," said Stretch, "I know where there's a MONSTER, just waiting to get you."

A Monster? Woffles began to shake all over again.

"Come upstairs," said Stretch. "I'll show you."

Up the stairs they went; Stretch,
followed by Muffy, followed by
Woffles.

"In there," said Stretch.

But that was the People's bedroom! They weren't allowed in the People's bedroom!

"We're n-not allowed to g-go in there," stammered Woffles.

"No," said Stretch. "And do you know why?"

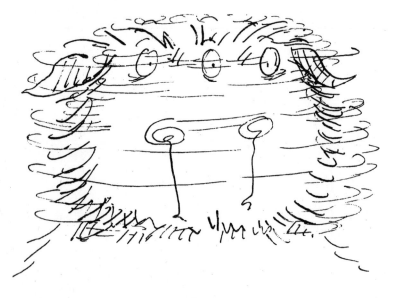

Woffles shook his head.

"It's because there is a big, fierce MONSTER living in there," said Stretch.

"Ho," said Muffy. "I'm not scared of any monster!"

"Is that so?" said Stretch; and he stre-e-e-e-tched up and opened the door. "Then I dare you to go in!"

Muffy hesitated.

"Scared?" said Stretch.

"Not me!" said Muffy. And she puffed herself up and went swaggering through the door. Into the People's bedroom…

Woffles held his breath. Stretch had a stre-e-e-e-tch.

Suddenly there was a
loud YOWL and Muffy
came tearing out. Her
hair was on end. Her tail
was in a frizz. She raced
past Woffles and hurtled
down the stairs. What could
she have seen?

"Come," said Stretch to Woffles. "Come and look!"

Woffles didn't want to. He was frightened!

"Hold on to my tail," said Stretch. "We'll go in together."

So into the People's bedroom went Woffles and Stretch.

"Look!" said Stretch.

Woffles took a deep breath. He opened his eyes. There in front of him…

…stood a BIG WOOLLY DOG!

CHAPTER FIVE

When the People came home they found Woffles curled up on the sofa. He was fast asleep.

Stretch was stretched out on top of the television. He was fast asleep, too.

It had been a busy day!

"Where is Muffy?" asked the People. "Muffy! Muffy! Where are you, Muffy!"

They found her in the kitchen. She was crammed against the wall, between the washing machine and the fridge. Her ears were pulled back. Her eyes were wide.

"Oh, poor Muffy!" cried the People. "What has happened? What has frightened you?"

Muffy couldn't tell them it was the monster that lived in their bedroom. A hideous horrible thing like a big furry football with pins sticking out of it.

Really sssssscary!

The People picked her up and carried her into the sitting room.

"There!" they said. "Go and cuddle with Woffles. He'll look after you!"

So Muffy crept up to Woffles and burrowed into his fur. She made a little nest, where she could feel safe.

And Woffles let her! He could have growled and said, "Go away." He could have snapped and said, "I don't want you!" But he didn't, because he wasn't that sort of dog.

Woffles wasn't frightened of Muffy any more. He had seen the big woolly dog in the People's bedroom. No wonder Muffy had run away! Any cat would run from a big fierce dog like that!

Now Muffy always cuddles up with Woffles on the sofa. Muffy and Woffles do everything together. They even woffle around the garden together.

As for Stretch… well! He just sleeps and eats and grooms and stretches. He never lifts a paw – why should he? He's the king of the house!

Printed by RR Donnelley at Glasgow, UK